THE

PASSOVER

by Rick Joyner

I.S.B.N. 1-878327-02-X

Distributed by:

MorningStar Publications, Inc.
P.O. Box 369
Pineville, North Carolina 28134

TABLE OF CONTENTS

INTRODUCTION

We may think of the Old Testament as the law and the New Testament as grace, but this is not necessarily true. If we read the New Testament with an old covenant heart it will just be law to us. Likewise, if we read the Old Testament with a new covenant heart we will see Christ, who is the righteousness of God. The Old Covenant is the *letter*; the New Covenant is the *Spirit*.

The Lord Jesus said, **"Do not think that I came to abolish the Law or the prophets; I did not come to abolish, but to fulfill. For truly I say to you, until heaven and earth pass away, not the smallest letter or stroke shall pass away for the Law, *until all is accomplished*"** (Matt.5:17-18). This does not mean that the Law will not pass away until we have kept all of the commandments as we are no longer under Law but grace. Matt.11:13 states that, **"The Law *prophesied* until John."** One of the primary purposes of the Law was to give a prophetic outline of the coming Messiah and the plan of God through history. It is in this sense that the Law as a prophecy will not pass away until what it has prophesied is fulfilled.

We see striking illustrations of the prophecies of the Law being fulfilled and then passing away in history. For example, after Jesus was crucified, the typical sacrifices of the Law which foretold this passed away so that they were no longer performed. When the church was birthed, which is the spiritual temple of God, the physical temple passed away shortly thereafter. We must see the Law as more than just the commandments and see it as a prophetic outline of history, the smallest letter of which is being fulfilled.

Paul instructed the Corinthians concerning Israel's exodus from Egypt, "Now these things happened to them as an example, **and they were written for our instruction, upon whom the ends of the ages have come"** (I Cor.10:11). There is understanding to be gained from the study of Israel's experience which is crucial for the church that will see the end of the age. This instruction is needed for the church to accomplish the mandate she has been given for this hour.

The first Passover delivered Israel out of her slavery to

Egypt and is a prophetic outline of how the cross would deliver the church from the power and bondage of the evil one for her own journey to her own Promised Land. The principles found in this can be applied to an individual, a church, or the international body of Christ.

This study is derived from the last chapter of the book There Were Two Trees In The Garden. We decided to expand this message into a separate book because of the importance of it for the time in which the church now finds herself. It is also a wonderful illustration of the manner in which the Law prophesied for the church "upon whom the ends of the ages have come," establishing many basic principles of interpreting this prophecy.

If you desire further study of this subject we would like to refer to the book There Were Two Trees In The Garden. This work begins in Genesis to establish a sound and comprehensive pattern for understanding the unfolding plan of God as seen in the Law and the prophets; the plan which culminates in the summing up of all things in Christ. There Were Two Trees In The Garden is the first of a series of seven books which will carry the reader on a prophetic journey from the Garden of Eden to the Promised Land, biblically, historically and, we pray, experientially. The second book in this series, The Journey Begins, is due to be released in 1990, with an additional volume to follow simi-annually.

To receive the most from this study please read Exodus chapters 1 through 12 before continuing.

THE SACRIFICE

Christ our Passover also has been sacrificed... (1 Cor. 5:7)

It was the Passover sacrifice which delivered Israel from the power of Pharaoh so that her people would never again serve Egypt. It is the cross, of which the Passover was a prophetic type, that delivers us from the power of Satan and slavery to the corruption of the world. Realizing this, Satan rages against those who turn to the cross just as Pharaoh did against Israel when he saw that he was losing his power over them. Like the Passover did in type, the cross brings judgement upon the evil of the world, but delivers those who embrace it from the world.

Since Cain and Abel, the sacrifice has been the main point of conflict between the two seeds, which represent the two natures of man--carnal and spiritual. Satan is not threatened if we embrace the doctrines or the institution of Christianity; in fact he may well encourage it. He knows that the good of the Tree of Knowledge is just as deadly as the evil, and far more deceptive. Human goodness is an affront to the cross, and is used as a compensation for it. It deludes us into thinking that if we do more "good" than evil we will be acceptable to the Father, thereby placing us above the need for the sacrifice of His Son. Satan may well encourage us to embrace anything religious as long as we do not turn to the cross. When we turn to the cross, Satan's power over us is completely broken; at that point we march out of his dominion into the glorious liberty of the Spirit--a relationship with our God.

The greatest opposition to one embracing the cross and the true liberty of the Spirit will be religious man. This battle began with the first two brothers, Cain and Abel, and rages to this day.

Cain was a type of religious man, who offered a sacrifice of grain, typical of his own works. The ground had been cursed because of the fall, and now it would only bring forth fruit by "the sweat of his brow." That is what Cain offered-- the fruit of his own toil. Abel was a type of those who seek

God's acceptance through the blood sacrifice. Cain's offering was rejected by the Lord, but Abel's was accepted. This enraged Cain, just as those who stand in the righteousness of the cross will always offend those who try to live by their own righteousness. Cain slew Abel because of this rage. This was a prophetic foreshadowing of the fact that it would be the self-righteous who would persecute and slay Jesus, and those who are born through His spiritual seed.

The cross will always be the greatest threat to religious man, and religious man will always be the greatest enemy of the cross. It was not the demon possessed who persecuted Jesus; they bowed the knee and submitted to Him. It was the religious, moral and conservative citizens who crucified Jesus, and these will be the ones to rise up against anyone who preaches the true message of the cross. The greatest persecution against the true faith will always come from those who have been converted in their minds but not in their hearts. These will be those who in fact live by the fruit of the Tree of The Knowledge of Good and Evil instead of the fruit of the Tree of Life. Their true devotion will be to intellectual comprehension of doctrines in place of a living relationship with God and compliance with His *will*.

As Jesus warned, **"Not every one who says to Me, Lord, Lord, will enter the kingdom of heaven; but he who does the will of My Father who is in heaven."** (Matt.7:21) We will only know true doctrine if we esteem doing His will *above* just knowing the doctrine, as He further explained: **"If any man is willing to do His will, he shall know of the doctrine, whether it is of God, or whether I speak from myself."** (John 7:17)

A person can desire truth for many different reasons, some of which are evil such as pride, self-justification or even fear. It is only those who have a love for the truth who will not be deceived in the evil day. Those who love the truth do want their doctrines to be accurate and pure. We will only have accurate and pure doctrines if we love the God of Truth more than the truths of God. It is not knowing the book of the Lord that gives life, but knowing the Lord of the book. If we love the Truth Himself more than we love the individual truths, we will love those truths more than we would if we esteemed them more than we do Him. It is not a matter of having one or the other, but having both if we have them in the proper order.

Satan often comes as "an angel of light," or *messenger of truth*, because it is one of his most effective strategies for keeping God's people in bondage. It is for this reason that the Lord did not say that we would know those who are His by how accurate their doctrines were, or the miracles that they did, but rather by their *fruit*. Satan knows and can quote the scriptures as well as any Christian, and he can counterfeit the gifts of the Spirit to a degree, but he cannot counterfeit the fruit of the Spirit. The fruit of the Spirit will always be of the Tree of Life, which is Jesus. When Satan uses scripture it is to get us to partake of the same fruit which he used to cause the fall of man--the fruit of the Tree of The Knowledge of Good and Evil.

Eve was not tempted by the evil from this tree, but the good; she was tempted by a desire for wisdom. If Satan cannot seduce us with sin, he will then try to seduce us with wisdom and knowledge which is acquired apart from God. This wisdom and knowledge always leads to self-righteousness and self-promotion because it is rooted in self-seeking, not in obedience.

The Lord wants us to have wisdom and knowledge, but it must be that which is motivated by seeking the glory and purpose of God, not our own ends, if it is to be of the tree which gives life. That's why we are exhorted to **"Study to show thyself approved unto God (*not men*)."** (II Tim.2:15 KJV) If we are studying to acquire wisdom and knowledge so that we can be more successful preachers, to prove our own positions and doctrines to dissenters, or for any reason other than the simplicity of devotion to Christ, then we are being beguiled by that wisdom and knowledge.

As Jesus explained: **"You search the scriptures, because you think that in them you have eternal life; and it is these that bear witness of Me."** (John 5:39) True life comes from the scriptures when they lead us to the Truth Himself, not just to truths, even accurate spiritual truths. True Christianity is not found in just getting our doctrines right, but in getting our relationship right, to Christ. We begin this relationship when we partake of the true Passover, the cross. Satan's

9

strategy is to use every means he can to keep us from it. Pharaoh's strategy to keep Israel in bondage is a parallel of the strategy which Satan still uses to keep men under his control and away from the cross.

As soon as Moses proclaimed liberty to Israel by the word of the Lord, Pharaoh countered by giving his men instructions to: **"Let the labor be heavier on the men, and let them work at it that they may pay no attention to false words"** (Ex.5:9). Pharaoh's strategy was to make the burdens on God's people heavier so that they would think that God's promises were "false words." Satan does the same to us; just before we are about to be delivered by the power of God he heaps the burdens on us to make us think that God's word is false.

This strategy against Israel began to work, causing them to doubt and become discouraged. To bring **DISCOURAGE-MENT** is Satan's first priority. If we are not ignorant of the enemy's schemes we will be prepared for them, and can combat them just as Moses did. If God gives you a promise, for example one of healing, Satan will immediately try to make you feel worse, thus getting you to turn from the promise of God as being false. We must learn to expect this attack when we receive the promise of God and not allow it to discourage us into thinking that His word is false.

After Moses and the people remained determined, Satan's next strategy was to duplicate the miracles of God. If the first tactic does not work, Satan will then try to make us think that there really is not anything special or unique about what God is promising, or that God's power is no greater than his. This is meant to bring disorientation. **DISORIENTATION** will be Satan's next tactic after he has been successful in sowing discouragement.

Because Moses remained determined, Pharaoh's next tactic was more cunning; he told them to **"Go sacrifice to your God within the land"** (Ex.8:25). When Satan sees that we are determined to serve the Lord, he will then try to make us think that we can serve God even though we remain under his bondage to the ways of this world. This is likened to the delusion that we can still maintain our former sins, but be forgiven as long as we go to church occasionally, or say that we are believers. Moses was not deceived, and neither must we be by this fallacy. After **DISCOURAGEMENT** and **DIS-ORIENTATION,** Satan's next weapon will be **COMPROMISE.**

When this tactic failed Pharaoh's next strategy was to allow them to go, but to get them to agree not to go very far. **"I will let you go, that you may sacrifice to the Lord your God in the wilderness; only you shall not go *far away"* (Ex.8:28).** This was Satan's attempt to get Israel to **LOSE HER VISION** for the Promised Land. This strategy has been most effective on many Christians. When we lose our vision we will just wander in the wilderness, making us easy prey for recapture. The call on Israel was not just to leave Egypt, but to go to the Promised Land. We must keep our vision on the ultimate purpose of God or we will be distracted by a lessor purpose.

When Moses remained steadfast to the call and vision of God, Pharaoh gave in a little but tried once more to get any measure of compromise that he could. He knew that if they compromised to any degree he would regain dominion over them. He told them that they could go as far away as they wanted and he only had one condition: **"Only let your flocks and your herds be detained. Even your little ones can go with you" (Ex.10:24).** This was another deadly diabolical trick. When Satan sees that we are utterly determined to "go all the way with Jesus" he then tries to get us to leave something behind. Satan understands very well that "Where your treasure is there will your heart be also." Compromise is spelled **D-E-F-E-A-T** for the people of God. We must be unrelenting in our determination to be utterly free of Satan's dominion over us or anything that is ours, responding like Moses, **"Therefore, our livestock, too, will go with us; NOT A HOOF WILL BE LEFT BEHIND!" (Ex.10:26).**

In this scenerio between Moses and Pharoah we have a lucid example of Satan's ancient strategy to keep God's people under his dominion. His first goal is to cause **DEPRESSION,** which leads to **DISORIENTATION,** then **LOSS OF VISION,** which leads to **COMPROMISE,** which brings **DEFEAT** to the purpose of God for His people.

Even with Pharaoh's defeat in implementing this strategy, he did not give up, and we should never expect Satan to release us of his own free will. Israel was not to be freed by the dictate of Pharaoh, lest he say that he had let them go.

Israel was only to be freed by the power of God. His power would bring destruction to the whole dominion of Pharaoh and give the treasures of Egypt into the hand of His people. We too must understand that we are not set free by the permission of Satan, or by our own steadfastness, but by the power of God. We too will spoil Satan's dominion when we uncompromisingly partake of the true Passover sacrifice of the Lamb.

Let us make straight paths for our feet, not turning to the right or to the left, and not compromising regardless of how reasonable the proposition may seem. In this way we will remain in the place where the power of the cross can work to bring us release, as well as bring judgement upon the dominion of the evil one.

A NEW BEGINNING

Now the Lord said to Moses and Aaron in the land of Egypt, "This month shall be the beginning of months to you; it is to be the first month of the year to you" (Ex. 12:1-2).

As the Passover was to be the archetypical prophecy of the sacrifice of Jesus, it is significant to note that Moses prepared Israel for the first Passover by rotating its calendar to a "first month". This heralded a new beginning. After partaking of the Passover the children of Israel were to leave the only place they had ever known, to travel through lands they had never seen, to possess a land about which they had only dreamed. Their life would never be the same after that one fateful day- -and neither is ours.

Therefore if any man be in Christ, he is a new creature: old things are passed away; behold ALL things are become new (2 Cor. 5:17, KJV).

When Jesus becomes our Passover, we are born again into a new world. To Israel it was a physical change; to us it is a spiritual change. The external conditions and surroundings may remain the same, but we do not. The externals appear different, but it is because our eyes are new! When one is born again he begins to see the Kingdom of God (John 3:3). This is a far more glorious deliverance. Moses led Israel out of Egypt in one day, but "Egypt" (the ways of the world) still remains in Israel. Through Christ "the world has been crucified to me, and I to the world" (Gal. 6:14). Jesus takes Egypt out of the heart and replaces it with a new country--the Kingdom of God. The seed of Cain, religious man, is forever seeking to make the world a better place in which to live. Christ changes men so that they might be better able to live in the world. The carnal man seeks to change men by changing the world. The spiritual man seeks to change the world by changing men.

Except for this tiny little pocket of darkness called earth, the glory of God prevails over the universe. Even through we are but a speck in the great expanse of creation, the Father made the supreme sacrifice to redeem and restore us by sending His own Son, to the overwhelming wonder of creation. But for this awesome fact, earth would register "zero" in significance compared to the expanse of God's dominion. When we begin to perceive the Lord and the dimensions of His dominion, personal, and even world problems begin to look insignificant. We can be sure that this one drop of evil will never overcome the oceans of His goodness. His kingdom will come! It is an irresistible force that will overshadow evil just as the sun overshadows the moon when it rises.

When man ate of the Tree of The Knowledge his attention became focused upon himself and he began to think of himself as the center of the universe. Every child born after the fall inherited this deception. Our little problems and ambitions completely dominate our minds until we are converted. Then, as we begin to see the Kingdom of God, our perspective is changed. The more clearly we see Him sitting on His throne, the less we notice the combined problems and cares of the world. Not that we do not care about them--we simply realize that He is so much bigger than any problem and more wonderful than any human ambition! As we see Him with new eyes we find a peace that is beyond comprehension. The world may not be one bit different, but we are.

Walking in truth is walking with God. As our vision of His kingdom is clarified, the things of earth do grow dim. The things that are invisible to the natural man become more real to us than things that are seen. To those who do not see in the spirit this sounds absurd. The apostle Paul explained it well:

But a natural man does not accept the things of the Spirit of God; for they are foolishness to him, and he cannot understand them, because they are spiritually appraised.

But he who is spiritual appraises all things (accurately), yet he himself is appraised by no man (1 Cor.2:14-15).

If we were to wake up and see Jesus standing beside our

bed, physically manifested, the day at the office would be quite different! How would the day change if He were to visibly accompany us to the office? To those born of the Spirit, "the eyes of the heart" see more clearly than the natural eyes. The Lord is with us wherever we go because He lives in us. When the eyes of our hearts remain open we will be beholding Him continually. That is reality--seeing Jesus in the power of His resurrection as the King over all rulers, powers and authorities.

When Stephen was martyred, he was not even distracted by the stones that were killing him. He was looking at Jesus! The apostle Paul, who was yet unconverted, witnessed the reality of Stephen's vision as he was being stoned. The Lord was even then preparing His chosen vessel to carry His name before the gentiles, kings and the sons of Israel. The seed that was planted in Paul's heart when he saw the reality Stephen lived in was to bear much fruit. Years later he wrote these penetrating verses about having the vision for this reality:

I pray that the eyes of your heart may be enlightened, so that you may know what is the hope of His calling, what are the riches of the glory of His inheritance in the saints,

and what is the surpassing greatness of His power toward us who believe. These are in accordance with the working of the strength of His might

which He brought about in Christ, when He raised Him from the dead, and seated Him at the right hand in the heavenly places,

far above all rule and authority and power and dominion, and every name that is named, not only in this age, but also the age to come.

And He put all things in subjection under His feet, and gave Him as head over all things to the church, which is His body, the fullness of Him who fills all in all (Eph. 1:18-23).

When Paul perceived Jesus on His throne, he saw all things subjected to Him. Jesus is still on the throne. All dominion has been given to Him and nothing can happen that He does not allow. It is impossible for Satan to sneak in a blow when Jesus is not looking. When the eyes of our heart are opened to see this, it is difficult to give much credence to the cares of the world. Elisha was another who had this vision. When confronted by an entire army, he sat peacefully on the side of a hill, much to his servant's dismay. When Elisha prayed for the servant's eyes to be opened, the servant was then able to understand the reason for Elisha's confidence; the angels standing for them outnumbered the enemy (see II Kings 6:8-23).

Walking in the Spirit is to see with His eyes, hear with His ears, and to understand with His heart. As we do this the earth with all of its problems and its glories starts to appear as small as it really is in the realm of the Spirit. After we have beheld the glory and authority of Jesus, kings and presidents are no more impressive than the wretched. Once we have seen the Lord all earthly pomp and position appears ludicrous, and the worst international crisis is hardly cause for concern. The King is on His throne, and He will never lose control.

When Isaiah saw the Lord sitting on His throne, there were seraphim with Him who called out to one another: "Holy, holy, holy, is the Lord of Hosts, *the whole earth is full of His glory*" (Is. 6:3). With all of the wars, conflicts, disasters, diseases, and confusion, how can the seraphim say that the whole earth is full of His glory? They are able to say it because they dwell in the presence of the Lord. As we begin to dwell in His presence, regardless of the circumstances, we too will see the whole earth as being full of His glory. We see the realities of what is taking place on earth, but we also see the greater reality of God's plan and power. We are citizens of the new creation, not the old, and we must see from the perspective of the new.

Now we might ask, if we are new creatures why do we have this continual battle with our old nature? We would not have this battle if we kept our eyes on Jesus. It is when we, like Peter, take our eyes off Him and focus on the tossing waves of the world and the flesh that we begin to sink. As Paul explained to the Romans:

> For I know that nothing good dwells in me, that is, in my flesh; for the wishing is present in me, but the doing of good is not.
>
> For the good that I wish, I do not do; but I practice the very evil that I do not wish.
>
> But if I am doing the very thing I do not wish, I am no longer the one doing it, but sin which dwells in me.
>
> I find then the principle that evil is present in me, the one who wishes to do good.
>
> For I joyfully concur with the law of God in the inner man,
>
> but I see a different law in the members of my body, waging war against the law of my mind, and making me a prisoner of the law of sin which is in my members.
>
> Wretched man that I am! Who will set me free from this body of death? THANKS BE TO GOD THROUGH CHRIST JESUS OUR LORD (Rom.7:18-25).

Without Christ, there is no good thing in us. No matter how many times we look at ourselves we will find the same thing--evil. But in Christ we no longer have to live by our sinful nature! He has given us His Life, His Spirit! When He said, "It is finished", He meant it. He is the finished work of God; He is the finished work the Father seeks to accomplish in us. Maturity is not accomplished by striving to reach a certain level of spirituality; maturity is simply abiding in Him Who is the finished work of God. Jesus *is* our wisdom, righteousness, sanctification and redemption (I Cor.1:30). Jesus is everything we are called to be; we can only be that which we have been called to be by abiding in Him.

We will never become the new creation we are called to be

by setting spiritual goals and attaining them. We can only attain true spirituality by abiding in the One who *is* the work of God. Jesus is the Alpha and Omega, the Beginning and the End of all things. Jesus is called "the first-born of all creation" (Col.1:15). Jesus is the whole Purpose of God. Everything that the Father loved and esteemed He brought forth in His Son. Everything was created *by* Him and *for* Him and in Him all things hold together (Col.1:16-17). The whole creation was *for* the Son. All things are to be summed up in Him (Eph.1:10). We accomplish the whole purpose of God in our life when we have our whole being summed up in Him by simply abiding in Him.

See to it that no one takes you captive through philosophy and empty deception, according to the tradition of men, according to the elementary principles of the world, rather than according to Christ.

For in Him all the fulness of the Deity dwells in bodily form,

and *in Him you have been made complete*...(Col.2:8-10)

We can, in our own strength, change our outward behavior to some degree, but only the Lord can change our hearts. We cannot even judge the thoughts and intentions of our hearts accurately, "For the heart is more deceitful than all else and is desperately sick; who can understand it?" (Jer. 17:9). We may have pretty good motives one day and terrible ones the next, about the same matter. If we only do things when our motives are right we will easily be foiled by Satan or deceived by our own hearts, even while we may have the best of intentions. If we allow our motives to control us we will be in perpetual confusion. Our lives must be determined by the will of God, not our motives. Paul explained this to the Corinthians:

But to me it is a very small thing that I should be examined by you, or by any human court; in fact, I do not even examine myself.

I am conscious of nothing against myself, yet I am not by this acquitted; but the one who examines me is the Lord (I Cor.4:3-4).

This does not mean that we ignore our problems, but we must depend upon the Lord's word to divide between soul and spirit. We are to "judge ourselves lest we be judged," but this must be done by the Spirit. Our judgement of ourselves can be distorted if it is not done by the Spirit. Our hearts are deceitful, and often we are more easily deceived by our own hearts than others are. We must depend on the Lord to change us if the change is to be real. We are changed as we behold His glory, not our own failings (II Cor.3:18).

But let us not be presumptuous; this does not give us license to follow evil motives. We are only to disregard our motives when they are in conflict with the will of God, not to pursue our own ends. Through Jesus, "He condemned sin in the flesh" (Rom.8:3). It is false doctrine which teaches God's grace as continual forgiveness for continual sin. When we abuse His grace and live after the flesh we have departed from grace.

He promised that we will never be tempted beyond what we are able to endure (1 Cor. 10:13). The grace that the Lord has given us is the **power** to walk by His Spirit. As Peter stated: **"Seeing that His divine power has granted (past tense) to us** *everything* **pertaining to life and godliness (God-likeness), through the true knowledge of Him"** (II Pet.1:3).

When we give in to the flesh, it is not because we do not have the strength to resist--we are simply giving in to sin! It's like training for the marathon. When the runner thinks he cannot go another step, if he will relax he will find that he can go a great deal further, and his endurance increases from that point. When we get to the point where we don't think we can stand the temptation any longer, if we will just rest in Him who has conquered all sin, we can endure far past the point at which we usually give up. It is at the point that we cannot stand it any longer that His strength takes over. **"My grace is sufficient for you, for My power is perfected in weakness"** (II Cor. 12:9).

Therefore, do not throw away your confidence, which has a great reward.

FOR YOU HAVE NEED OF ENDURANCE, so that when you have done the will of God, you may receive what was promised.

"For yet in a little while, He who is coming will come, and will not delay.

But My righteous one shall live by faith; and if he shrinks back, My soul has no pleasure in him."

But we are not of those who shrink back to destruction, but of those who have faith to the preserving of the soul (Heb.10:35-39).

The athlete's endurance does not increase until he reaches the previous limit of his endurance and overtakes it. The same is true of our spiritual endurance. We can testify with Paul: "I can do all things through Him who strengthens me" (Phil. 4:13). In Christ we can never say "can't" to what He has called us to do. We can say we that we "will not" or "did not," but we can never say that we "can not." He has given us *His* strength.

In Him you were circumcised with a circumcision made without hands, in the removal of the body of the flesh by the circumcision of Christ. (Col.2:11)

There is therefore now no condemnation for those who are in Christ Jesus.

For the law of the Spirit of life in Christ Jesus has set you free from the law of sin and death.

For what the Law could not do, weak as it was through the flesh and as an offering for sin, He condemned sin in the flesh (Rom. 8:1-3).

The Lord is not just trying to change us; He is trying to *kill* us! The ultimate high calling of God is attained when we can say with the apostle, "I have been crucified with Christ; and it is no longer I who live, but *Christ lives in me*; and the life which I now live in the flesh I live by faith in the Son of God, who loved me and delivered Himself up for me." Gal. 2:20)

John the Baptist was a wonderful type of true spiritual ministry. His whole purpose and devotion was to prepare the way for Jesus, to point to Him, and then to decrease as He increased. He did not say that he would decrease *so that* Jesus could increase, but he said Jesus "must increase, but I must decrease" (John 3:30). If we try to decrease *so* Jesus can increase we are still pursuing a self-righteousness by which we try to dictate His increase. Again, it is as we see Him and His glory that we are changed into His same image (II Cor. 3:18). Only then will there be a true decrease of our own self-life. To presume that we can crucify our own flesh is vanity. If we were to crucify ourselves, all that we would have left is self-righteousness. We do not crucify ourselves, but rather we are crucified *"with Christ."*

The new birth is possibly the greatest demonstration of the love and grace of God. We have all sinned and are worthy of eternal destruction. But the Father so loved us that He sent His own Son to be a propitiation for our sins, allowing us to start all over again. We exchange our body of death for eternal life as the Lord's own children. No genius of fantasy or fiction could have ever dreamed a more wonderful story. How could we who have partaken of such glory not "do all things for the sake of the gospel" (I Cor.9:23)?

For the love of Christ controls us, having concluded this, that one died for all, therefore all died;

and He died for all, *that they who live should no longer live for themselves, but for Him,* who died and rose again on their behalf.

Therefore from now on we recognize no man according to the flesh; even though we have known Christ according to

21

the flesh, yet we know Him thus no longer.

Therefore if any man is in Christ, he is a *new creature*; the old things passed away; behold new things have come.

Now all these things are from God, who reconciled us to Himself through Christ, and gave us the ministry of reconciliation,

namely, that God was in Christ reconciling the world to Himself, not counting their trespasses against them, and He has committed to us the word of reconciliation.

Therefore, we are ambassadors for Christ, as though God were entreating through us; we beg you on behalf of Christ, be reconciled to God.

He made Him who knew no sin to be sin on our behalf, that we might be the righteousness of God in Him. (II Cor.5:14-21)

TAKING THE LAMB INTO THE HOUSE

> Speak to all the congregation of Israel, saying, "On the tenth of this month they are each one to take a lamb for themselves, according to their father's households, a lamb for each household...And you shall keep it until the fourteenth day of the same month" (Ex.2:3,6).

The purpose of taking the lamb into the house five days before the sacrifice was to carefully examine it for flaws. This was a prophecy that Jesus, the true Passover Lamb, would enter Jerusalem five days before His crucifixion, which He did, perfectly fulfilling the Word. While He was entering the city the ritual Passover lambs were themselves being taken into the houses. As these lambs were being examined for disqualifying flaws the scribes, Pharisees, and Sadducees were challenging Jesus trying to find a flaw in Him. None was found; He was the acceptable sacrifice for God's Passover. The rulers finally resigned themselves to hiring false witnesses against Him.

In John 19:42 we note that Jesus was slain on the Jewish Day of Preparation. On this day all the Passover lambs were slain to prepare for the feast. As Jesus was nailed to the cross, knives were being put to the throats of sacrificial lambs throughout Israel. The fulfillment of the type was taking place right in their midst.

Even His own disciples did not understand what was happening. Do we yet understand what has happened? Jesus alone is the Lamb who is without blemish. We may know this in our minds, but do we yet believe it in our hearts? How is it that we still judge our ability to be accepted by the Father by how well we are doing, instead of the *only* way that we have become acceptable to Him, by the blood of His Son. Our ability to come boldly before the throne of grace must never be measured by how good or bad we have been, but by the blood of Jesus; any other motive is an affront to that cross.

If we are being obedient in order to become acceptable we are being an affront to the cross which alone has gained our approval with God. True ministry does not come in order to gain God's approval, but it comes from a position of *having* His approval, because of the Lamb. We are obedient because we have been bought with a price and we no longer belong to ourselves, but to Him who has purchased us with His own life. We love Him because He first loved us. We now labor because we love Him for *the price He paid* to gain our acceptance, and we long to see Him receive the reward of His sacrifice. There is a difference between trying to please God because we love Him and we want to bring Him joy, and trying to please Him in order to be acceptable. The former is worship; the latter is still the self-seeking pursuit of self-righteousness.

Our failure to understand this aspect of the Passover may well be an answer to why there has been such a superficial nature to modern conversions. Major, international evangelists confess that less than twenty percent of those who make a decision in their crusades go on to walk with the Lord. Could it be that there is something lacking in the gospel we preach? Could it be that instead of trying to get such hasty "decisions" we would serve men better if, like Israel, we encouraged them to take the Lamb into their "houses" for a few days before they embrace the sacrifice? Would the decisions not be more real if men were encouraged to first examine Jesus thoroughly so that they would know for themselves that there is no flaw in Him?

There are times when a person is ready to make a decision and be reborn immediately. But generally, some of our modern evangelistic methods are not bearing fruit that remains. In the parable of the sower, the Lord said that, **"When anyone hears the word of the kingdom, *and does not understand it*,the evil one comes along and snatches away what has been sown in his heart"** (Matt.13:19). Likewise, He said, **"The one on whom the seed was sown on the good soil, this is the man *who hears the word and understands it.*"**(verse 23).

There are times when we need to heed the biblical exhortation to not lean on our own understanding (Prov.3:5), but not at conversion. Those who make a commitment because of hype, or emotional stimulation, or even at the prompting of anointed preaching, are in danger of having the seed snatched away if they do not understand it. If one is inclined to trust an issue as significant as eternal life to something he does not understand, is it even possible that he has believed in his heart?

As precious as redemption, salvation and the purposes of God are, one who has truly believed in his heart will be compelled to sink his roots as deep as possible into these matters. True faith is not blind; it is illumination in the most profound sense. True faith has nothing to fear from examination; it has everything to gain. There is a difference between believing in the mind and believing in the heart, but they are not mutually exclusive. If we are truly examining Jesus, and not just intellectual concepts, the more closely we look at Him the more our hearts will be stirred to believe. Even Napoleon, after reading the gospel of John, stated that if Jesus was not the Son of God then the one who wrote that gospel was!

There was a time when Jesus asked His disciples who men said that He was. They answered "Some say John the Baptist; some, Elijah, and others Jeremiah, or one of the prophets." (Matt.16:14) He then challenged them, "But who do *you* say that I am." (verse 15). If they were to be true disciples they could not be following Him because of who others said He was. The same is true with us. It is not who our pastor says He is, or our favorite author, teacher or televangelist. Sooner or later that finger has got to be pointed right in our own chest--"Who do *you* say that the Son of Man is!" We cannot be converted to another man's Jesus; He has got to be *our* Jesus.

When Peter answered the Lord's question that He was the Christ, the Son of God, the Lord replied, "Blessed are you, Simon Barjona, because flesh and blood did not reveal this to you, but My Father who is in heaven." (verse 17). Peter was obviously not moved by what others thought of Jesus; he was open to receive his own revelation. When we are open to receiving our own revelation from the Father, like Peter, we are building upon a rock that the gates of hell cannot prevail against. One can teach a parrot to say the right things and do the right things, but it will never be in it's heart. If our understanding is simply the parroting of another, it is not true understanding, it is not in our heart, and it will never stand the test which surely comes upon every seed that is planted.

This is not meant to be an attack upon particular evangelist's methods. Like Paul, we should rejoice that Jesus is being preached even if the results are not perfect. Even if just twenty percent are converted that is still a great many who may not have been reached had these men not been out there doing what they were doing. But there is wisdom in the biblical pattern of having those who would partake of the Passover sacrifice examine the Lamb thoroughly before doing so. We will not lose any true converts by doing this; we may gain many.

HE WAS CRUCIFIED BY US ALL

The WHOLE ASSEMBLY of the congregation of Israel is to kill it (the lamb) at twilight... (Ex.12:6).

And ALL THE PEOPLE answered and said, "His blood be on us and on our children" (Matt.27:25).

As prophesied, it was the whole congregation of Israel that delivered Jesus to be crucified. Yet it was not just Israel that crucified Him; it was the carnal nature of man that is within us all. Had the Lord chosen any other nation to send His Son to, there would have been the same results. Even Plato perceived that a truly righteous man would be despised by all men and eventually be impaled (the Greek equivalent of crucifixion). True Christians have always been persecuted, and are still persecuted in almost every nation of the world. The Lord Himself declared, "As you have done unto the least of these brothers of Mine you have done it unto Me." (Matt 25:40) Jesus has completely identified Himself with those for whom He died. If we have ever persecuted, slandered, or brought injury upon any of His, we have done it to the Lord himself. If we have betrayed a congregation, a minister, or a brother, even one who is the least, even one who is in doctrinal error or has other problems, we have betrayed the Lord Himself.

Let us not continue casting stones at others who fall short of God's glory because we have also fallen. When we judge another servant, or congregation of the Lord we are in fact judging Him. What we are saying when we judge another one of God's sheep is that His workmanship does not meet up to our standards, and that we could do it better.

When the people rose up against Moses, his reply was that they were not rebelling against him, but against God. (Ex.16:8) Moses did not mean by this that he was perfect, or that everything he did was perfect, but that he was the one God had appointed as the leader. If Israel rebelled against Moses they were saying that God did not know what He was doing by appointing him.

The same may be true of our tendency to judge leaders or even circumstances. If we are critical of a person or the circumstance the Lord has us in, we are in fact saying that we do not think the Lord knows what He is doing in ordering our life. We are not just judging the circumstance, we are judging God. The same may be true if we are judging our spouses, families, or superiors. How can we trust the Lord with our eternal salvation if we can not trust Him in the everyday matters of life? Of course, there are cases where we are in the wrong job or other circumstance. Then we should be preparing for a change, not by being critical, but with faith and a joyful heart, praying for the situation or people we are leaving.

Let us never be so foolish as to be critical of God and His workmanship. It was because of their *grumbling* and *complaining* that the first generation to leave Egypt perished in the wilderness. It is for the same reason that many of us never leave the wilderness, we have been placed in for temporary training. If we lack faith like Israel in the wilderness we go around and around the same mountain of trial; only when we begin to believe God will we be able to leave.

Possibly the greatest reason for the church's lack of light, power and a closer relationship with the Lord is her critical spirit. The Lord directly addressed this through the prophet Isaiah:

Then your light will break out like the dawn, and your recovery will speedily sping forth; and your righteousenss will go before you; the glory of the Lord will be your rear guard.

Then you will call, and the Lord will answer; you will cry, and He will say "Here I am." *IF you remove the yoke for your midst, the pointing of the finger, and speaking wickedness.* **(Is.58:8-9)**

The Lord here promises light, restoration, righteousness, the glory of the Lord and answered prayer if we remove the yoke of the critical spirit (pointing of the finger and speaking wickedness). As if we needed even more motivation than this to repent of this evil, Jesus gave it to us:

Do not judge lest you be judged.

For in the way you judge, you will be judged; and by your standard of measure, it shall be measured to you. (Matt.- 7:1-2)

We have seen this so often fulfilled. Those who set themselves up as judges to criticize others with different views or doctrines end up becoming stumbling blocks, doing more damage to the church in the name of truth than many do with error. A stumbling block is the very last thing one would want to be as the Lord warned:

It is inevitable that stumbling blocks come; but woe to him through whom they come!

It would be better for him if a millstone were hung around his neck and he were thrown into the sea, that that he should cause one of these little ones to stumble. (Luke 17:1-2)

In addressing the Corinthian problem of immorality, Paul asked "Do you not judge those who are within the church?" (I Cor.5:12). Those in leadership do have the authority and the responsibility to judge those who are within the church, but there is a certain biblical pattern which must be followed. This judgement can almost always be distinguished from that which is coming from stumbling blocks by how it complies with the biblical wisdom for judging within the church. First we are commanded to go to the person we believe is in sin or error alone. *If* the person does not repent, we are then to take another with us to entreat him further. Only if the person fails to repent after this is it lawful to bring the issue before the church (see Matt.18:15-17).

The Lord's command as to the manner in which we are to reprove those who are in error was given immediately following His exhortation about the stumbling blocks. Those who go public with their accusations without complying to this mandate have almost certainly placed themselves in jeopardy of being stumbling blocks, regardless of how accurate their judgement is.

Even if we comply with the Lord's mandate in this we can still be in error if we do it in the wrong spirit as Paul warned the Galatians:

> Brethren, even if a man is caught in *any* tresspass, you who are spiritual, restore such a one in a spirit of gentleness; looking to yourself, lest you too be tempted. (Gal.6:1)

It is no accident that those who go public with their judgement of others end up falling publicly. Those who write books in the spirit of the "accuser of the brethren" are soon consumed with spiritual paranoia and darkness of heart. The repercussions for speaking in a critical spirit about a brother are bad in this life but even more terrible when we stand before the Lord's judgement seat. Those who measure out judgement will have it measured back to them in the same measure. Those who show mercy will receive mercy; those who give grace will have the same. As we are all in desperate need of mercy and grace, let us be devoted to being vessels for the same.

> But I say to you that every one who is angry with his brother shall be guilty before the court; and whoever shall say to his brother, "Raca," shall be guilty before the supreme court; and whoever shall say, "You Fool," shall be guilty enough to go into the fiery hell.
>
> If therefore you are presenting your offering at the altar, and there remember that your brother has something against you,
>
> leave your offering there before the altar, and go your way; first be reconciled to your brother, and then come and present your offering. (Matt.5:22-24)

Some have misconstrued this text to justify going to a brother that they have something against, but that is not what it is saying. We are compelled to forgive those who may have wronged us, but we are asked to go and make right what someone may have against us. In this we are commanded to show mercy, *but not expect or require it from others*. What they do in this is between them and the Lord; we are to be concerned only with ourselves. This may seem unfair but the Lord does not mean for it to be fair. If we want what is fair we have all sinned and are worthy of death! Every chance we have to forgive and show mercy or grace is a great opportunity to receive more mercy and grace from the Lord. But when we show mercy or forgive, let us do it secretly before the Father that He may reward us. When we do this in a way so as to receive recognition we have received our reward by that recognition.

There was a wonderful story related about a South Pacific culture where it was the custom of men to trade cows for a wife. A father might receive two cows for an average daughter. An above average girl would usually bring her father three cows. Only a rare beauty would ever bring four cows. There was a father here with a daughter so homely he was hoping he could get even one cow for her. There was another man on the island who was considered their most astute trader. To everyone's astonishment, this man came and offered eight cows for this father's homely daughter! Everyone thought the wise trader had lost his mind, but it was not long before this homely girl was transformed into the most beautiful and gracious woman in the land. She had started to think of herself as an eight cow woman, and she became one!

We determine the value of a commodity by what someone is willing to pay for it. What were we bought with? What was our wife, husband, child, parent, friend or boss bought with? The most precious commodity in all of creation was paid for them--the blood of the Son of God. We must begin knowing one another after the Spirit, and seeing each other as God does. When we do this we will begin to see as dramatic a change in some as there was in the homely young girl from the South Pacific. We must stop crucifying the Lord again in each other, but begin esteeming the Lord and His workmanship in each one, giving the value to one another which He gave. Few things will work to the edification of the whole body of Christ so much as our starting to know each other after the Spirit instead of after the flesh. Let us pray to only see with His eyes, hear with His ears and understand with His heart. Then we will be the most astute and wise men in the land.

> **Therefore, thus says the Lord, "If you return, then I will restore you—before Me you will stand. *And if you extract the precious from the worthless, you will become My spokesman*" (Jer.15:19).**

When we start to see the precious in that which appears worthless, and begin speaking to it and drawing it out of one another, we will start to become the prophetic people we must be to accomplish the mandate of God for this hour. Let us stop crucifying Christ again when He comes in even the least of His little ones, but start recognizing Him, honoring Him and calling Him forth in one another.

Like the Pharisees in the first century, many Christians are usually looking for Jesus on His white horse, conquering and reigning, even when they are looking for Him in His people. This is truly His state in heaven, but if we want to see Jesus in His people we sometimes have to have the heart of Simeon and Anna. They were able to see in a mere infant the Salvation of the whole world. We are sometimes so busy looking for the fruit we fail to see the seed that is to become the fruit. Let us be discerning enough not to miss Him in whatever form He appears. True wise men will worship Him even in His infancy. True apostles are yet in labor that He might be formed in His people. True prophets are always looking for the One they are called to point to and acknowledge, preparing His way and making it straight.

THE BLOOD MUST BE APPLIED

Moreover, they shall take some of the blood and put it on the two doorposts and on the lintel of the houses in which they eat it (Ex. 12:7).

The angel of death could not touch the houses that had the lamb's blood applied to them. Without the blood they would have been doomed to the same judgement that came upon Egypt. It is by the application of the blood of Jesus to our lives that we are freed from God's judgement against the world and its sin, the wages of that sin being death. Nothing more, or less, will save us.

It would not have done Israel any good to know that there had to be the sacrifice of the Passover lamb, or even to sacrifice it, *unless they also applied it's blood to their houses.* Likewise, it will not benefit us to just know that there had to be a propitiation for our sins; it will not even do us any good to know that Jesus made that propitiation, *unless His blood is applied to our life.* To just know facts without applying them accomplishes nothing. Even demons know and believe the doctrine of salvation. It is not knowing in our minds, but believing in our hearts, which brings salvation (see Rom.10: 9-10).

The Lord explained through Moses that "the life is in the blood" (Lev. 17:11). It is only by the application of the Life of Jesus to our lives that we are saved: "We were reconciled to God through the death of His Son, much more, having been reconciled, WE SHALL BE SAVED BY HIS LIFE" (Rom. 5:10). The simple recognition of historic facts or understanding spiritual principles does not accomplish this; His life must be applied to our lives.

Because knowledge has so often been substituted for life, many have been made to feel comfortable in a spiritual condition in which they remain lost. Just having knowledge does not mean that it has been applied. Thomas a'Kempis wrote, "I would rather feel contrition than know the definition thereof... For what good does it do a man to be able to discourse profoundly concerning the Trinity, but lack humility and thereby be displeasing to the Trinity?"

There has been a great increase of knowledge during these last days, including spiritual knowledge. It has come because we are going to need every bit of it to accomplish the mandate the Lord has given us for this day. But the substituting of knowledge FOR life has led to much of the shallowness and lack of power in the church today. Knowledge only puffs up unless it leads to transformation and life. The Way is not a formula, but a Person. Truth is not just the assimilation and comprehension of spiritual facts, but a Person. Unless we have come to know Jesus as our Life we do not really know the Way or the Truth either.

The miracles performed by the Lord were not done just to impress us with His power; they were also meant to convey a message. His first miracle is the first one we need to understand. By it He was showing His newly gathered disciples the initial work to be done in them. At the wedding at Cana, the Lord ordered the vessels set aside. These vessels were typical of the disciples. He then had them filled with water, which is typical of the Word of God. Then He turned that water into wine, testifying of the fact that the Word would be changed into Spirit and Life. Once we have tasted this wine we will never again be satisfied with mere water. He has some who have allowed Him to fill them to the brim, and even then they have not gone out to serve it; they have waited patiently until the Lord has turned that water into the finest wine. This is what Paul meant when he said that "when it pleased the Father to reveal His Son *in me* (not just *to* him) then I preached" (Gal.1:16).

Paul explained how the blood was applied to his life when he declared: "I have been crucified with Christ; and it is no longer I who live, but Christ who lives in me" (Gal. 2:20). Salvation is more than just forgiveness for sinful actions; it is deliverance from the indwelling evil that causes those actions! The crucifixion of Jesus accomplished an exchange for us--our body of death for His resurrection life. It is true we must die to our lives, interests and will to partake of Him; but no creature in all of creation will ever make a more profitable transaction.

WE MUST EAT THE FLESH

And they shall eat the flesh the same night, roasted with fire, and they shall eat it with unleavened bread and bitter herbs (Ex. 12:8).

Jesus therefore said to them, "Truly, truly, I say to you, unless you eat of the flesh of the Son of Man and drink His blood, you have no life in yourselves.

He who eats My flesh and drinks My blood has eternal life; and I will raise him up on the last day.

For My flesh is true food, and My blood is true drink.

He who eats My flesh and drinks My blood abides in Me, I in him.

As the living Father sent Me, and I live because of the Father, so he who eats Me, he also shall live because of Me" (John 6:53-57).

"We are what we eat" is a common axiom. If we are partaking of the Lord Jesus, the Tree of Life, we will become that Life. Jesus did not say "he who has eaten My flesh," but "he who *eats*". This speaks of our need to continually partake of Him to abide in Him. He is the true Manna from Heaven (John 6:58). Just as Israel had to gather fresh manna each day because it would spoil if stored, so we too must seek Him afresh each day. We cannot be sustained on day old revelation. We cannot set aside one day to be spiritual and expect to abide in Him the rest of the week. He must be new to us every morning.

When the Lord referred to the eating of His flesh and drinking of His blood, of course He was not talking of His physical flesh and blood, but of what they symbolically represented--His life and His body, the church (We are bone of His bone and flesh of His flesh). Perplexed by what He said, most of those who heard this departed from Him (John

6:66). Confused leaders of the Church later reduced this truth to the destructive ritual of the Eucharist. What Jesus refers to is a *reality*, not just a ritual. To partake of the ritual is not equivalent to partaking of Him. The ritual of the Lord's supper was given as a reminder, not a substitute. When this ritual usurped the reality, the very life of the Lord was removed from the church, and she then plunged into the Dark Ages--an appropriate title for the spiritual depravity of those times.

The apostle Paul explained the meaning of this ritual to the Corinthians: "The cup of blessing which we bless, is it not the communion of the blood of Christ? The bread which we break, is it not the communion of the body of Christ?" (I Cor.10:16 KJV). Communion was originally two words which were merged to form one--COMMON and UNION. This translates from the Greek KOINONIA, which is defined as: "The using of a thing in common." It is not the bread and wine that brings us together, but what they symbolically represent--the blood and body of Jesus. The ritual we call communion is not an actual communion; it is a symbolic testimony that those partaking of it have a common - union in Christ. Jesus is our communion. He binds us together. The ritual simply designates the Purveyor of the bond. As Paul warned the Corinthians:

For I received from the Lord that which I also delivered to you, that the Lord Jesus in the night in which He was betrayed took bread;

and when He had given thanks, He broke it and said, "This is My body, which is for you; do this in REMEM-BRANCE of Me".

In this same way He took the cup also, after supper, saying, "This cup is the new covenant in My blood; do this, as often as you drink it, in REMEMBRANCE of Me."

For as often as you eat this bread and drink the cup, you PROCLAIM the Lord's death until He comes.

Therefore, whoever eats the bread or drinks the cup of the Lord in an unworthy manner, shall be guilty of the body and blood of the Lord.

But let a man examine himself and so let him eat of the bread and drink of the cup.

For he who eats and drinks, eats and drinks judgment to himself if he does not judge the body rightly.

For this reason many among you are weak and sick, and a number sleep (1 Cor.11:23-30).

If we do not discern the body of Christ rightly we are pronouncing judgement upon ourselves when we partake of the bread and wine. That is, if we participate in the ritual assuming it fulfills our obligation to commune with Christ, we have deceived ourselves; we remain deprived of true Life. The substitution of rituals for realities has pervasively deprived men of redemption and salvation. "For this reason many are weak, and sick, and a number sleep." If a member of our physical body was cut off from the rest of the body it would become weak, sick and die very fast. The same happens when we cut ourselves off from our spiritual body, the church. As the apostle John declared: "If we walk in the light as He Himself is in the light, we have fellowship (Greek "Koinonia": communion) with one another, and the blood of His Son cleanses us from all sin." The Lord said "the life is in the blood". If we have "communed" with Him, we are joined in one Body under the Head, and His life's blood can flow through us.

Being properly joined to the body of Christ is not an option if true life is going to flow through us. But let us not substitute being joined to the body with being joined to the Head. By many, modern, popular definitions of what it means to be joined to the body, it has become possible, and even common, to be joined to the body without even having a relationship to the Head. Much of the church's emphasis over the last half of the twentieth century has been on being joined to the body, with very little emphasis on our being joined to the Head. If one is properly joined to the Head he will be properly joined to the body also, but the reverse is not necessarily true. We must not continue to get the cart in front of the horse in this issue.

Of course there have been many to use the excuse that they were seeking the Lord to avoid having a relationship to the church. As Peter related that "the unstable and untaught" distort teaching as well as the scriptures, there will be many who distort even the most sound doctrine. This is not an "either/or" issue. We must esteem our personal relationship to the Lord first, and also be properly related to His body if we are to have life. He said that we must "eat His flesh" *and* "drink His blood."

WE MUST EAT THE WHOLE THING

Do not eat any of it raw or boiled at all with water, but rather roasted with fire, both its head and entrails. And you shall not leave any of it over until morning...(Ex. 12:9-10).

Some have become very particular about the gospel; as if it were up to them to choose the aspects of redemption they need. If we are to partake of the Lord's Passover, we must accept every part of Him. He did not give us the option to take what we want. As He stated in the parable, when we find the pearl of great price, we must buy the whole field in which it was found.

When the Lord commissioned His followers to go and make disciples of all nations, He specifically included "teaching them to observe **ALL** that I commanded you" (Matt. 28:20). When we come with preconditions of what we will accept, we void the very power of the gospel. Often it is that which represents the greatest threat to us that we need the most.

The specific matter that intimidates us is not the important issue; to pick and choose what WE want is an abdication of His Lordship. He cannot be received as Savior unless He also comes as Lord. It is the abdication to His Lordship that delivers us from the self-centeredness that kills us. Those who claim to have received Him as Savior but continue to live according to their own will are deceived. True salvation is the deliverance from self-will and our self-life, in exchange for His life. If He is not the Lord *of* all He is not the Lord *at* all.

When we compromise the gospel to make it acceptable, or for any other reason, we strip it of the power to save. Deliverance from the power of evil is not accomplished by making a few changes. It is accomplished by deliverance from the "I WILL" that is rooted in our fallen nature, and the continual attempts we make to build our own towers to heaven.

Satan's original and most successful temptation has been that we could be "like God" (Gen. 3:5). Man's most destructive error is his determination to be his own lord! The whole world esteems and emulates "self-made" men. If one is self-made he has thwarted his purpose for existence, to *be made* in the image of his Creator. Self-made men are supreme failures. "What will it profit a man to gain the whole world and lose his soul?" The Passover sacrifice of Jesus did not just "paint over" us with His blood; it cleansed us to destroy the angel of death, the body of sin, our self-will. Any gospel that preaches salvation without complete surrender is without salvation as well, and is an enemy of the true gospel. A compromised gospel only immunizes us to the truth so that we cannot receive it when it comes to us.

"For whoever wishes to save his life shall lose it; but whoever loses his life for My sake shall find it" (Matt. 16:25).

If we want His life we must be willing to share His death. When the Lord called a man, he had to leave everything: **"So therefore, no one of you can be My disciple who does not give up all of his own possessions"** (Luke 14:33). Whether He requires this of us literally, or just in our heart, it must be real and total. He will either be Lord of all or not at all. We must all experience the lessons of Job who had to lose everything but the Lord before he knew that the Lord was all he needed. A man who stands in need of nothing but Jesus will not be bound by anything or anyone but Him.

The Church today is fragmented. We have assumed the freedom to choose for ourselves which parts of the body of Christ we will accept. We naturally gravitate toward that which is most comfortable. The result has been a debilitating imbalance in most congregations. Those with an evangelistic burden are found in one group; those with a pastoral burden in another; the prophets in still another; one congregation is all "feet," another "hands," another "eyes". These bodies are grotesque substitutes for the perfect body Christ is determined to have. Each member must be properly joined to the others if the Body is to function rightly. Even if one is a perfect heart, what good would that heart be if it did not have the lungs, kidneys, liver, etc. Presently we have all hearts in one place claiming to be the body, all livers in another, and so forth. There must be interchange, interrelationship, and the proper joining of the different parts of the body before there can be an effective functioning of the same.

Pastors have a God-given cautious nature that is protective of the flock of God. Prophets are by nature visionary. Without the balance and influence of the prophetic ministry, pastors will tend to stagnate and become set in their ways. Without the influence of pastors, prophets will drift into extremes, having visions which no one knows how to practically fulfill. Teachers will be pragmatic in nature, which is essential for clear impartation of the word, but without prodding from the other ministries they tend to reduce the life in Christ to principles and formulas that are learned by rote. Evangelists are given to focus on the needs of the lost, often forgetting to raise and mature them--but without evangelists the Church will quickly forget the unsaved. Because apostles are called to be evangelists, prophets, pastors and teachers, they usually have a more balanced nature, and are given for the purpose of keeping the Church on the right path. The unity of the Spirit is not a unity by conformity; it is a unity of diversity. For this reason the Lord gave apostles, prophets, evangelists, pastors and teachers to equip the saints (Eph. 4:11-12). We must receive *all* the ministries. To partake of the Lord's body we must "eat the whole thing".

We are exhorted to "grow up in *all* aspects unto Him, Who is the Head" (Eph. 4:15). The apostles were directed to "speak to the people in the temple the *whole* message of this Life" (Acts 5:20). The psalmist discerned that "the SUM of Thy word is truth" (Psalm 119:160). We can be distracted from the Truth by individual truths. We can be distracted from the River of Life by the individual tributaries which feed it. Almost every denomination is built around a single emphasis. They may teach other aspects, but emphasize one small portion of the whole revelation of God. Any time we focus our attention on one part of the whole, our scope will be limited. Only when we focus on the Truth (Jesus) do all truths take their proper perspective. Jesus is the Sum of God's word.

Until we see Jesus as the summation of all spiritual truth, we are like the proverbial blind men trying to comprehend the elephant: one thought it was a tree because he had found its

41

leg; another thought it was a fan because he had found an ear; another thought it was a whip because he had found the tail, and so it goes. When we see the whole animal we understand that they were all correct, but in fact would be deceived about the true nature of the elephant until they perceived the whole thing. Individual aspects of God's word may be interpreted falsely apart from the whole Word. The Lord emphasized the fact that the scriptures have eternal life in them only if they testify of Him (John 5:39-40). Overbalance in one area is indicative of partial, incomplete comprehension of the whole. As Paul explained to the Hebrews: "God, after He spoke long ago to the fathers in the prophets in many portions and many ways, in these last days has spoken to us **in His Son**" (Heb. 1:1-2). The Father is no longer giving us fragments. He has given us the whole Loaf.

We may have such a vision of the united and perfected Body of Christ that we are sure this Church will draw all men to itself. But the church is not to draw men, but to minister to them and equip them once they have been drawn. It is only when Jesus is lifted up that men will be drawn together, and they will be drawn to HIM! King David perceived this and wrote the "Psalm of Unity" (Psalm 133): "Behold how good and pleasant it is for brothers to dwell together in unity! It is like precious oil UPON THE HEAD (Jesus), coming down upon the beard...coming down upon the edge of his robes". If we anoint the Head with our worship and devotion, the oil will run down and cover the whole body (of Christ). There will one day be a Church that is perfected in unity, but it is likely that she will not even be aware of it. Her attention will be on Jesus, not herself.

Now you shall eat it in this manner: with your loins girded, your sandals on your feet, and your staff in your hand; and YOU SHALL EAT IT IN HASTE (Ex.12:11).

Included in the Passover was The Feast of Unleavened Bread (Ex.12:14-20). For seven days (beginning with the first day of the Passover) Israel could not eat any leavened bread. This was meant to remind the Israelites of their flight from Egypt, when they left in such haste their bread did not have time to become leavened:

And they baked the dough which they had brought out of Egypt into cakes of unleavened bread. For it had not become leavened, since they were driven out of Egypt and could not delay (Ex.12:39).

Because of its permeating characteristics, leaven (yeast) is symbolic of sin in scripture:

Do you not know that a little leaven leavens the whole lump of dough?

Clean out the old leaven, that you may be a new lump, just as in fact you are unleavened. For Christ our Passover also has been sacrificed.

Let us therefore celebrate the feast, not with old leaven, nor with the leaven of malice and wickedness, but with the unleavened bread of sincerity and truth (1 Cor. 5:6-8).

Leaven is also symbolic of doctrine that is legalistic in nature. The Lord warned His disciples to "Beware of the leaven of the Pharisees and Sadducees" (Matt.16:6). Not long after the gospel began to spread, converts from the Pharisees tried to bring the young Church under the yoke of the Law. Satan was trying to seduce the young bride of Christ with the same deception used to seduce the bride of the first Adam: eat of the Tree of The Knowledge of Good and Evil. After great controversy, the apostles and elders sent word to all of the churches in what was a most important and historical communique.

> For it seemed good to the Holy Spirit and to us to lay upon you no greater burden than these essentials:
>
> that you abstain from things strangled and from fornication; if you keep yourselves free from such things, you will do well (Acts 15:28-29).

Webster's New World Dictionary defines leaven as "A substance such as yeast used to produce fermentation, especially in dough". The same dictionary defines fermentation as "A state of excitement; agitation; commotion; unrest." The apostles and elders in Jerusalem noted that the Pharisee converts produced the same characteristics in the Church: "Since we have heard that some of our number to whom we gave no instruction, have *disturbed* you with their words, *unsettling* your souls" (Acts 15:24). Such are the characteristics of spiritual leaven.

Doctrines that disturb and unsettle the body of Christ are often rooted in legalism. There is a continual pressure upon the Church to walk in principles and/or formulas to gain maturity. These doctrines usually seem "good for food, a delight to the eyes, and desirable to make one wise" (Gen.3:6). Satan could not tempt us if the fruit were not appealing. Laws, principles and formulas are appealing because they offer the security of a known commodity. Walking by law or principles gives us the control that our insecurity demands. But this is a false security. It is security in oneself rather than the One in Whom alone there is true security.

"For all who are being led by the Spirit of God, these are the sons of God" (Rom.8:14). As discussed earlier, walking by the Spirit does not mean that we do not keep the Law. If we walk by the Spirit we do more than keep the Law; we fulfill it! For example, the law says we are not to covet our neighbor's wife or property. The Spirit calls us to an even higher way, to love our neighbor. If we love our neighbor, of course we will not covet what is his, or in any way do him harm. The Spirit does not just command; He imparts the ability to love...He imparts His love. Jesus did not come to destroy the Law but to fulfill it--He came to lift us **above** the Law; He came to give us the power to exceed its requirements.

Walking in the Spirit is life, peace and fulfillment, but it is difficult. It is difficult because the flesh wars against the Spirit. The "I WILL" nature of Cain within us will not easily submit to the Spirit. There is a determination in the flesh to "be as God"; to rule its own destiny. This determination to control desperately resists relinquishing control. But if we are to live by the Spirit, Jesus alone must be our Master.

It is easier to make rules than to be sensitive to the Spirit. Regulations can bring order and relieve many pressures, but they cannot change the inner man. A time is coming when the regulations will not be able to cope with the chaos. We must have a more solid foundation. If we are seeking order and security in our religion we will lose both.

The fear of deception will not keep one from deception, it will lead to it. We cannot walk by fear, but by faith. The scripture testifies that the only thing that will keep us from deception is to have a *love for the Truth*, Himself. When we open our shades at night, darkness does not come in, light shines out into the darkness. Light overcomes darkness because it is more powerful. If we seek to do our Father's will and serve Him, we will find an order and security that no degree of chaos can overcome. We must be able to hear and distinguish His voice from all the other voices in the world. When the shaking comes, and it will (Heb.12:25-29), knowing His voice and following Him will be the only true security we have, and it is the greatest security we can have.

Does this mean that we should do away with all laws, rules, and regulations in society? Certainly not! As the apostle explained: "But we know that the law is good if one uses it lawfully, realizing the fact that the law was not made for the righteous man (those in Christ), but for those who are lawless and rebellious, for the ungodly and sinners, for the unholy and profane" (I Tim.1:8-9). In the world, laws and regulations are necessary to retain a semblance of order until the kingdom comes, but they must not be imposed for spiritual discipline; only the Spirit can beget that which is spirit.

The Bible is God's instruction book for the human being. It contains the greatest wisdom ever written in the human language. It gives important instructions about how the human really works, concerning both our potential and what causes our problems. It would be impossible to put a value on this most marvelous gift the Lord has given to us, but the Bible was given to lead us to Jesus, not to take His place.

The Lord says amazingly less than one would think concerning order in the Church (for a good reason). It is essential for His sheep to know His voice. The Church must be ruled and guided by the Head rather than by formulas. He is purposely vague concerning even important issues so that we have to seek Him. The New Testament is full of the best counsel the world has ever heard, but the Lord and His apostles were careful not to lay down many general rules and regulations for the churches. They knew that every rule could prevent that church from seeking the Lord for themselves.

Developing the relationship with Him is the important work that the Spirit is doing in us. He was sent to lead us to Jesus. Used as a rulebook, the Bible becomes the letter that kills, the Tree of Knowledge, and can even become an idol. Used properly, it turns us to Him, helps us to walk with Him, abide in Him, and know Him, not just about Him.

The Pharisees confronted every problem with a new rule. The Lord referred to their doctrines as leaven because they caused agitation and commotion among the people. When we try to confront problems in the Church with new regulations we are sowing leaven. Like the doctrines of the Pharisees, these only clean up the outside; they are not able to deal with the true problem. They may bring a degree of control and order, but the greatest order one can find among people is in the cemetery! When order takes the place of having a relationship with the Lord that is usually what we end up with--a spiritual cemetery. The dead don't cause any problems. The spiritually dead will have an orderly church. But the Lord came to give ABUNDANT life. Abundance does not dictate that it be all good; it just means there is a lot of it! It includes the good and the bad.

Living by regulations will give outward order but it will

breed agitation and unrest in spirit. There is no true rest in the law until there is death, making men machines or zombies instead of humans who are able to have a relationship with their Creator. Jesus is "the Lord of the Sabbath", or the Lord of rest. Abiding in Him we have Life and peace. He says to us: "Cease striving and know that I AM God" (Ps.46:10). The Law makes us look at ourselves where we will only see death and corruption. The Spirit shows us Jesus and Life which creates a love and yearning that keeps us always in pursuit of Him.

"The unfolding of Thy word gives light" says the Psalmist (Ps.119:130). There is unfathomable depth of revelation we have not yet realized in God's Word, even concerning the most basic doctrines. It is a terrible mistake to become satisfied with our present knowledge and understanding. We all are seeing through a glass darkly. We cannot know anything fully until we know Him fully. "The path of the righteous is like the light of dawn, that shines brighter and brighter until the full day" (Prov.4:18). When the truth stops expanding for us we begin to live in darkness.

Water is often used symbolically as the Word of God in scripture (see Eph.5:26). When the Lord uses a natural type to symbolize a spiritual reality, it is because its characteristics reflect the nature of the spiritual. One important characteristic of water is that it must keep flowing in order to stay pure. Once it settles into one place it becomes stagnant very fast, and so does the Word of God. Every revelation of truth in our life should be continually expanding and deepening for us. That's why the river of life is just that--a river! It is not a pond or a lake; it is flowing, moving, going somewhere. As an old sage once remarked, "You can never step into the same river twice."

Having truth that expands is threatening to those who are of the spirit of the Pharisees: who do have a zeal for the Lord and desire for purity of truth but whose real security is in fact in human traditions with which they insolate the truth. With those who are of this spirit, there will be a defacto elevating of orthodoxy to the same level as biblical revelation, even though they would vehemently deny that this is so. When we understand that there is much more to be understood, and we are seeking deeper understanding concerning a doctrine, there *is* the potential for erroneous revelation. If we do not seek deeper revelation we already have error that is debilitating and poisonous. **Having truth will not keep one from deception, but having *a love for the truth* will.**

Israel's bread did not have time to become leavened because they left Egypt in such haste. If we too will keep moving on with the Spirit, our bread will not have time to become leavened with sin, wickedness, or legalism. It's when we stop moving and growing that our "bread" becomes infected.

In the chapter "Taking The Lamb Into The House," we discussed how the Passover lamb was taken into the houses of Israel to be thoroughly examined for five days before the sacrifice, and how this may reflect the need for one to thoroughly examine Christ before making a commitment. But we see here, once the commitment is made we must then move in haste to flee the land of Egypt.

It is interesting to note that *immediately* after one believed in the early church he was baptised. This speaks of the need not to force or rush a decision out of a person, but once a true commitment is made, it needs to be sealed at once with the biblical ordinance given for the public demonstration of faith--water baptism. Nowhere in scripture do we find such things as an altar call, the raising of hands, or the myriad of other customs we have substituted for the biblical rite of immediate baptism. These human devices, which have been instituted mostly for the sake of convenience, have proven counter-productive in sealing the commitment of the new believer. How much more impact would the "decision" have on new converts if we faithfully complied with the biblical mandate for immediate baptism. How much more would their commitment stand as a powerful road mark in their lives if they could see a biblical testimony of their action, in place of the vague wonder if anything really happened after a walk down an isle or the brief raising of their hands?

NO STRANGERS MAY EAT OF IT

This is the ordinance of the Passover: NO STRANGER MAY EAT OF IT (Ex. 12:43).

As the Church grows in the grace and knowledge of our Lord we will become more tolerant, but this does not mean we will be all-inclusive. History testifies that each restoration of truth to the church is vulnerable to getting diluted or stamped out by the multitude. Our tendency to seek security through the approval of numbers has cost the church immeasurably by watering down the power of the pure and uncompromised truth. We are warned to beware when all men think well of us. Did people not heartily hail the false prophets? (Luke 6:26) We must be secure only in the justification and approval of God. "The fear of man is a snare" (Prov. 29:25).

A door has two functions: to let people in and to keep them out. Jesus is the Door. When we allow those to join the church who have not come through the Door we place both the congregation and the unconverted in jeopardy. This is not to say these should not be allowed to attend services or meetings, but that they should not be included as a member of the Body of Christ until they have been joined to the Head.

New buildings, family life centers, projects and programs, have drawn many into the churches. They may have also helped to keep some in churches, but they have never drawn a man to Christ. We may even think that the dynamic spirituality of our fellowship will bring men to Him, but it never will. The church can actually be a distraction and hindrance to true conversion if it allows membership in the church without rebirth in Jesus. Mere church attendance and activism can work to appease the conviction the Holy Spirit is seeking to bring into one's life, and may enable one to feel safe in a spiritual condition in which he remains lost.

The first thing which God said was NOT GOOD was for man to be alone. He made us social creatures and therefore we all crave strong social ties. The true Church is the most dynamic social entity the world has ever known. We must be

49

careful that people are not drawn to our assemblies instead of to the Lord. It is common for people to say the right things, change their outward behavior and even sincerely believe the doctrine of Christ in their minds but without knowing Jesus in their heart. It is possible to be quite "spiritual" and not know Him, as the Lord Himself testified.

Many will say to Me on that day, "Lord, Lord, did we not prophesy in Your name, and in your name cast out demons, and in Your name perform many miracles?" And I will say to them, "I never knew you; depart from Me you who practice lawlessness" (Matt. 7:22-23).

"The branch cannot bear fruit of itself, unless it abides in the vine, so neither can you unless you abide in Me" (John 15:4). To be joined to the Church through Christ is life and power. Seeking union with Christ through the Church is vain. One cannot be joined to Christ without being joined to His Body. We have often made it easy for one to be attached to the body without being joined to the Head. Paul scrupulously presented Christ crucified to the unsaved. He understood that if people were drawn by anything but Jesus the conversion could be false. Paul used no psychology or methodology. He used something much more powerful--*the gospel*.

There is great danger in "not discerning the body rightly" and allowing those to join with us who have not come through the Door. It is also dangerous to presume knowledge of another's spiritual condition or his standing before God when it is not *obvious*. There are certain basic truths we must agree on in order to walk together, essentially the atonement and Lordship of Jesus. When we become exclusive based on our doctrines which go beyond the revelation of Jesus as the Door, we are in danger of cutting ourselves off from the Body of Christ, and becoming a sect or even a cult.

The Tabernacle of Moses was a type of both the Lord Jesus and the Church, as both were to be the habitation of God. In Moses' Tabernacle, the closer one came to the presence of the Lord, the more sanctified he was required to be. Our situation is similar. The apostle exhorts: **"Pursue peace with all men (tolerance), and the sanctification**

redemption
restitution

50

(separation) without which no one will see the Lord" (Heb. 12:14).

When the Tabernacle of Moses was constructed and sanctified for use, an unsanctified man could not enter the Holy Place or even look upon the furniture inside. The penalty for this was death (Num.4:20). This was to testify of the requirement of sanctification before we can see the most holy things. If one is living in darkness and is suddenly exposed to great light, he will not be enlightened, He will be blinded! Because of this we must be discerning when exposing unbelievers, or new believers, to the deeper truths of the Lord. Meat will not nourish babies; it will choke them.

Because acacia wood was twisted, knotty and hard to work with, it is often typical of fallen human nature in scripture. In the Outer Court of the Tabernacle of Moses the furniture was made of natural, exposed, acacia wood and was illumined by the natural light of the sun. This testified of the fact that most who just enter the Outer Court usually have their sinful nature exposed and walk more by the "natural" light.

Entering the Tabernacle we come into the Holy Place. The furniture here is made of acacia wood, but it is covered in pure gold. Gold, being incorruptible, is symbolic of the Divine nature. The only light in the Holy Place is provided by olive oil burned in a lampstand, the olive oil being typical of the anointing of the Holy Spirit. In the Holy Place there is no natural light, and we cannot function there with our natural minds but are dependent on the Holy Spirit. In the Holy of Holies, the innermost compartment where the Lord Himself dwells, the mercy seat is gold inside and out. The light provided in the Holy of Holies is the very Presence of the Lord. We see by this that the closer one gets to the glory of the Lord the more gold there is, typifying the fact that we are changed into the Divine nature by the glory (see II Cor.3:18). As we get closer to the glory, the light by which we walk changes from natural light, to the anointing of the Holy Spirit, to the very presence and glory of the Lord.

"Our God is a consuming fire" (Heb.12:29). Had the acacia wood been exposed to the fire of God's glory without being covered by the gold, it would have been consumed. Sanctification is required to see the Lord and to draw close to Him, for our sake, lest we be consumed (Heb.12:14).

Unfortunately, many have a concept of the Father as being the God of the Old Testament who would destroy us if Jesus did not mediate and assuage His wrath. We must not forget that it was the Father who sent His Son because He "so loved the world." The Father Himself loves us, and desires fellowship with us so much that He submitted His own Son to torture and death so that we could draw near to Him. But God is holy, and His holiness is a consuming fire. That is why sanctification is required to see Him; if we are still wood, hay and stubble, we will be consumed by His presence. It is only as we have come to more fully abide in His Son, being covered by more and more of the gold of His divine nature, that we are able to draw closer and closer to the Father. It was the crucifixion of Jesus that rent the veil which separated us from the Father. It is as we are "crucified with Christ," when His cleansing blood has been applied to life, that the way is made for us to boldly enter into the Father's presence which is the heart's desire of our Father.

The ministry in the Outer Court is to the people. The ministry in the Holy Place and Holy of Holies is to the Lord. This is what transforms us. Without this ministry to the Lord we will not be as effective in our Outer Court ministry. We must carry light from the Lord, but we cannot take the people into that light until they have been sanctified. No strangers may partake of the Passover of the Lord, and one who has not discerned the Body rightly should not partake of the bread and wine.

Just as there were three dimensions to the tabernacle ministry, the Lord had three basic levels to His ministry: to the multitude, the twelve and then the three. He spoke to the multitudes in parables and basics (the Outer Court). To the twelve He revealed the mysteries, and they experienced the anointing (Holy Place). The three were priveleged to see His glory on the Mount of Transfiguration (Holy Of Holies). Pastors who are evangelical in orientation will have congregations which focus mostly on the Outer Court aspect of the ministry. Pastors who are teacher oriented will tend to have congregations which emphasize the ministry typified by the Holy Place. Those led by prophets will seek to abide in the

Holy of Holies. The properly balanced congregations will have a ministry on all three levels as the Lord and the tabernacle exemplify.

Every congregation and minister needs to have an outreach to the lost and ministry to those at every level of maturity. Failure to do so usually leads to imbalance and often error. If we do not have new converts, there will be stagnation. If we do not have meetings that are devoted entirely to worshipping the Lord without the distraction of human pressure, demands, and even needs, there will be shallowness and a lack of anointing and power for the ministry to the people.

Recognizing the importance of providing ministry for all levels of maturity is essential, but we must understand that it is wrong to distinguish and value people by their level of maturity. The purpose for each level of ministry was to prepare those in that place for the next higher level. If the ministry is functioning properly everyone will be maturing and entering higher levels of experience, effectiveness and intimacy with the Lord Himself. Those in ministry need to discern where a person is in order to serve him effectively, not to label him as a certain class of Christian.

Some have taken this understanding of the levels of maturity to classify and distinguish themselves as superior, or others as inferior. This cannot be helped. As Peter remarked concerning Paul's teachings, there were some things in them which were hard to understand, which the unstable and untaught distorted, just as they did the rest of the scriptures (see II Pet.3:15-16). Pride in a man's heart will cause him to use even the scriptures to feed his ego. If true humility is in one's character, even the greatest accolades of God and man will but further humble him.

True humility is not an inferiority complex. True humility comes from seeing the majesty of the Lord. As the apostle explained, those who measure themselves by themselves (or with each other) were without understanding (II Cor.10:12). In His kingdom the purpose of authority and position is for serving. The faithful and obedient ministry of helps is more esteemed with God than the most noteworthy apostle who considers himself higher than others.

There will be tares growing among the wheat in the

church. Even the apostle Paul ordained elders who would prove to be wolves (see Acts 20:29-30). Jesus chose Judas and included him in the inner circle. Though these may cause great damage and confusion, they are actually working out the purposes of God. All things work for the good of those who love God. Such disruptions almost always result in our becoming more dependent on the Lord, and less on those who are but flesh and blood. This is not to say we should purposely ordain traitors and include false brethren in our assemblies, but that it will happen and it will work out for our good.

During the 1960's and 70's there was a major emphasis upon "submission" in the Body of Christ. This was a word from God and only He knows how badly we needed it because of the rebellion then surfacing in the world. But we quickly formed our doctrines on submission and started judging men by how well they conformed to the doctrine instead of looking for the fruit of submission in their lives. As a result of this, some of the most unbroken and rebellious ministries were released upon the church because they conformed to the doctrine of submission. Likewise, some of the most truly broken and submissive men and women of God were almost blackballed from ministry because they did not conform to the doctrine. The devastation caused by this shallowness is now history.

In the coming years, "humility" will become an emphasis. This is a timely and important word, but let us not make the same mistake with it that we did with submission. The Lord does resist the proud and gives grace to the humble, but it is so much better when we let Him do it. We must start to know one another after the Spirit and not after the flesh. Only the Spirit can judge accurately. Appearances are almost always deceiving. King Saul appeared humble; it was said that he was "small in his own eyes." David appeared arrogant and insolent, rebuking the armies of Israel for their timidity and saying that the King's own armor was not good enough for him. We must rise above the tendency to follow the first one who appears to be head and shoulders above the rest.

Those whom we judge as tares by our own understanding may well be wheat and vice versa. That is why the Lord instructed us to let the wheat and tares grow together until the harvest. Until there is maturity, the wheat and tares may look so much alike that it will be almost impossible to tell them apart. Both may be arrogant; they may both even have false concepts or teaching, or fall into sin occasionally. The difference will only be obvious when they both mature. During the harvest wheat will bow over, while the tares remain standing upright; when wheat matures it becomes humble, but those who are in fact tares will continue in their pride.

Let us also not forget God's grace or judgement. Some who are tares may repent and become wheat. Likewise, some who are wheat will fall and become stumbling blocks in our midst. That "no strangers are to partake of the Passover" is a truth, but let us be careful how we apply it. Those who have not entered through the Door are obvious. Judging beyond that is difficult and dangerous, and can lead to grievous errors.

If we are walking in the Light we will allow truth to remain at the point of Divine tension between the extremes, and will refrain from making a formula, principle, or inflexible doctrine out of it. It is the fruit of the Tree of Knowledge which demands our carrying the paradoxes in scripture to their logical conclusions. The paradoxes are there to force us to seek the Lord for His mind and wisdom. This leads to our walking by the Spirit instead of principles or laws. By resisting the compulsion to make formulas and allowing truth to rest at the point of tension between the extremes, we begin to partake of the Tree of Life. Christianity is not just following a set of rules, it is walking with God.

SPOILING EGYPT

Now the sons of Israel had done according to the word of Moses, for they had requested from the Egyptians articles of silver and articles of gold, and clothing;

and the Lord had given the people favor in the sight of the Egyptians, so that they let them have their request. Thus they plundered the Egyptians (Ex. 12:35-36).

After being slaves for four hundred years, after Israel partook of the Passover, they became more wealthy than their wildest imagination could probably have conceived. When we partake of the true Passover, Christ, in Him we are given the right to become the sons of God to Whom belongs the world and all it contains. Even so, all of the world's riches are as nothing compared to the spiritual riches that are in Christ. But just as it is written, "Things which eye has not seen and ear has not heard, and which have not entered into the heart of man, all that God has prepared for those who love Him" (I Cor. 2:9). Truly, in Christ we have inherited more riches than we are capable of imagining.

Israel left Egypt weighted down with wealth, but they were not taken to the closest bazaar so they could spend it. He took them into the wilderness where they could not spend even a single shekel! There they were able to invest their riches for something more valuable than anything the world could sell them--the tabernacle, a habitation for God that He might dwell among them.

Today the Body of Christ receives a great deal of teaching about the riches we have in Christ. This teaching is timely. For centuries the Church has been deprived of the inheritance she has in Christ. Unfortunately this emphasis has often been devoted more to the material than the eternal. This is the delusion of slaves who one day dramatically find themselves kings. We have been removed from Egypt but Egypt has not yet been removed from us in many ways. However, it is encouraging that many are beginning to reject this mentality and envision the incomparable riches of Christ.

Blessed be the God and Father of our Lord Jesus Christ, who has blessed us with every *spiritual blessing* in the *heavenly places* in Christ (Eph.1:3).

When we perceive our spiritual blessings in Christ, material blessings lose their appeal. If one were to discover a vein of gold that could provide all the world's needs forever, would he continue panning for mere nuggets? We have that vein in the Person of our Lord Jesus. Why do we give so much attention to the things which pass away? Because we have not truly seen Him as He is; we have merely discovered a few things about Him.

In Hebrews 11 (popularly referred to as "the faith chapter"), there is a long list of the great triumphs of faith. These are wonderful testimonies of God's faithfulness to those who call upon Him in faith. Many deliverances are taking place today that are just as wonderful. But seldom is the last part of that chapter noted:

And others were tortured, *not accepting their release, in order that they might obtain a better resurrection*;

and others experienced mockings and scourgings, yes also chains and imprisonment.

They were stoned, they were sawn in two, they were tempted, they were put to death with the sword; they went about in sheepskins, *being destitute, afflicted, ill treated,*

men of whom the world was not worthy, wandering in deserts and mountains and caves and holes in the ground.

And all these, having gained approval through their faith, did not receive what was promised,

because God had provided something better for us, so that apart from us they should not be made perfect (Heb.11:35 -40).

These who were seeking a "better resurrection" did not
quench the power of fire or close the mouths of lions, they
would not even accept their release! They did not live in
palaces; they lived in holes in the ground and in caves. The
Lord Jesus Himself did not even have a place to lay His head
(Matt.8:20). When we begin to see the spiritual riches in
Christ, it will not matter to us where we live. If Jesus is in
it, a cave will have more glory than the greatest human
structure. To live in a cave or palace will make little difference if we abide in Him. Some think it is more spiritual to
be abased, others that it is more spiritual to abound, but
neither is true. We may be in error if we are trying to live
an abased life and God has not call us to it, or vice versa.
The issue is to be in the will of the Lord, and to keep a
steadfast devotion to Him whether we are abounding or being
abased.

Cain was the father of those who are earthly minded; he
was a "tiller of the ground." Those who are still carnal will
always be seekers of earthly gain, regardless of the spiritual
guise. The Kingdom of our Lord and His chosen is not of this
world. Those who seek His kingdom are strangers and
sojourners; here they have no lasting city and they are not
trying to build one; they are seeking the city whose architect
and builder is God.

This heart of the spiritual sojourner cannot be attained by
seeking it. Those who seek to be unearthly for its own sake,
believing it to spiritual, usually become sad examples of
spiritual barreness. "The promises of God are, in Him, yea,
and amen." (II Cor.1:20) The promises of God are positives,
not negatives. A failure to understand this is why some of the
most worldly and unspiritual men are found in monasteries
and secluded spiritual communities. (This is not to imply that
all who are found in these are so.) The truly spiritual man is
one because his heart is so captured by the things of the
spirit that he simply has no time or interest for the things of
the world. Once we have beheld the spiritual riches that are
found in Christ going back to worldly interests could be
compared to a billionare sweeping streets for minimum wages.
Those who still have a love for worldly pleasures simply have
not received the love of the Father (see I John 1:15). As Paul

explained to the Colossians:

> If you have died with Christ to the elementary principles of the world, why, as if you were living in the world, do you submit yourself to decrees, such as,
>
> "Do not handle, do not taste, do not touch!"
>
> which all refer to things destined to perish with the using, in accordance with the commandments and teachings of men?
>
> These are matters which have, to be sure, the appearance of wisdom in self-made religion and self-abasement and severe treatment of the body, *but are of no value against fleshly indulgence.* (Col.2:20-23)

True spirituality is not just a distaste for the world and its interests; true spirituality is a consuming love for the things of the Spirit and the interests of our God. This can only come when the eyes of our heart have been opened so that the things of the Spirit are more real to us than the things which are seen with the eyes of our minds.

THE WAVING OF THE SHEAF

As a fitting last touch to this remarkable Feast of the Passover, the Lord instituted what is called "The Waving of the Sheaf of the Firstfruits." (see Lev.23:5-15) This feast was celebrated in early spring as the first first shoots of the coming harvest were just sprouting. On the morning after the Passover Sabbath, a sheaf of this first evidence of the coming harvest was brought to the priest and he waved them before the Lord. As this ritual was being performed after the Passover of our Lord's crucifixion, Jesus was bursting forth from His tomb! Jesus was the Sheaf of the firstfruits of the resurrection, who at that very time was being waved before the Lord as evidence of the coming great harvest, perfectly fulfilling the type.

It is an interesting fact that more scripture is devoted to Abraham choosing a burial place for his family than on such important subjects as being born again or church order. Issac and Jacob insisted on being buried there, and Joseph made the sons of Israel swear to carry his bones up from Egypt to bury Him there. It is a great enigma as to why the patriarchs give so much importance to where they are to be buried until we read Matt.27:50-53.

And Jesus cried out again with a loud voice, and yielded up His spirit.

And behold, the veil of the temple was torn in two from top to bottom, and the earth shook; and the rocks were split,

and the tombs were opened; and many bodies of the saints who had fallen asleep were raised;

and coming out of the tombs *after His resurrection* they entered the holy city and appeared to many.

The burial ground which Abraham had chosen for his family was just outside of Jerusalem. Abraham was a prophet who had foreseen the resurrection of Jesus as the Lord Himself confirmed, "Your father Abraham rejoiced to see my day; and he saw it and was glad." (John 8:56) Abraham and those of his family who had vision had made a provision to be a part of the first resurrection.

The patriarchs were not just concerned about where they were buried but when they would be raised. Those who have vision are also making provision by how they are buried as to how they will be raised. If we have been buried with Christ we shall also be raised with Him (Rom.6:5). Every Christian is called to be a martyr--everyday! We make provision for our resurrection every day by laying down our lives and being buried with Him. In the light of this, one of the great men of vision of all time gave the church what may be his most important exhortation:

> For we are the true circumcision, who worship in the Spirit of God and glory in Christ Jesus and put no confidence in the flesh...

> More than that, I count all things to be loss in view of the surpassing value of knowing Christ Jesus my Lord, for whom I have suffered the loss of all things, and count them but rubbish in order that I may gain Christ,

> and may be found in Him, not having a righteousness of my own derived from the Law, but that which is through faith in Christ, the righteousness which comes from God on the basis of faith,

> that I may know Him, and the power of His resurrection and the fellowship of His sufferings, being conformed to His death; in order that I may attain to the resurrection from the dead.

> Not that I have already obtained it, or have already become perfect, but I press on in order that I may lay hold of that for which also I was laid hold of by Christ Jesus.

> Brethren, I do not regard myself as having laid hold of it

yet; but one thing I do: forgetting what lies behind and reaching forward to what lies ahead,

I press on toward the goal for the prize of the upward call of God in Christ Jesus (Phil.3:3, 8-14).

When Paul declared *"one thing I do,"* it reflected the singleness of his mind on this issue. When our eye, or vision, is likewise single, our whole body will be full of light. Only then will we know true resurrection life and power.

To receive a free catalog of the books and tapes distributed by MorningStar Publications, send your request to:

M.P.I.
P.O. Box 369
Pineville, NC. 28134

To receive <u>The Morning Star</u> Prophetic Newsletter, send a requested donation of $5.00 or more to the same address. If you cannot afford to send a donation, please send your request anyway. We would like to send it to you as a gift.